SKATEBOARDING IS NOT A BOOK

VERNON ADAMS & GAVIN HILLS

Mediabrats in cultural suicide

FANTAIL PUBLISHING,
an imprint of Puffin Enterprises

Published by the Penguin Group,
27 Wrights Lane, London W8 5EQ
England

First published 1989

0140 900284

13579108642

Printed and bound in

Great Britain by

William Clowes Limited,

Beccles and London

Designed by Dave Crook

PHOTOS: Tim Leighton-Boyce
Paul Sunman
Tim Ridley
Santa Cruz Skateboards
Powell Peralta

RAMP PLANS: Dan Adams

Acknowledgements: Shane O'Brien, Ian Lawson,
Steve Keenan, Gavin O'Brien, Jim Fitzpatrick,
Nick Philips, Joe Evans, Jason Florio, Darryl,
Cynthia Rose, Slam City Skates, R.A.D. Magazine, God,
and anyone else who knows me . . .

> "The principle by which each slight variation,
> if useful, is preserved, I have termed Natural
> Selection."
> *The origin of the species, ch 3, Charles Darwin.*

The skateboard will probably never be ranked as one of the great human achievements of the 20th Century, and skaters past and present are never likely to receive the accolades society bestows upon other better-known athletes and artists. Expect no gallery retrospectives, and no presidential receptions – instead pride yourself on nearly 30 years of your family history . . . your **Roots**! Through the boom-death boom-death-boom beat, the eternal rise and fall of the skateboarding movement, someone has always been skating. Skateboarding has as rich and lively a history as the youth culture that spawned it – a history rich in creativity, consumerism, and conflict – so expect no lists of olympic golds, no top tens and no boulevard named Peralta.

Understand, please, that the skateboard was not invented – no date, no time. It came into being through a process of evolution, and the proverbial ape that stood up was the roller-skate-board.

– '50s America, cinema neons shouting alien films into a cold war sky and Jailhouse Rock thudding from the milkbar where rollerskating waitresses deliver double cheeseburgers to hip Fonz clones. A waitress slips on a stray pickle, showering all and sundry with blueberry milk and the David Crocket special and a roller skate sends two wheels flying across the room.

Roller skates, like shoes, are seldom useful unless in a pair, yet broken roller skates had their uses. Kid brothers enjoyed banging roller skate wheels onto cut-off planks. They stuck a pole on the front with a cross bar to hold and made 'scooter-carts', the earliest recognisable forerunner to the skateboard. The carts provided weekends of fun but not much variety. To find the skateboard as we know it, we must travel onward to the early '60s.

California, two girls for every boy, surf's up and blond haired buddies are making waves. Yet some days the sea is like a lake, so there's no fun in the sun and it's too early to *"Turn on, tune in, drop out"*. Kid brother's scooter cart is broken. The front pole and crossbar have come off. Your surfer's instinct tells you to ride it. You lean left, you turn left; you lean right, you turn right; you catch a kerb not a wave, but "sidewalk surfing" is born.

In 1964 early planks had become boards and the first organised commercial skateboards had come onto the market. One of the first skateboard companies was Makaha. Situated in the back of Surf-Guide magazine, they made surfboard-shaped solid ash blanks and laminated dark and light striped hardwood decks. Surfboard manufacturers Gorden and Smith (G&S) also turned their lathes to skateboard manufacture and are the only original company to have survived.

There appeared to be a limitless market for this new creation. By the end of '64 teams were cropping up everywhere, and surf sound supremoes Jan & Dean were top of the charts with *"Sidewalk Surfing"*. This legendary song can boast the first vinyl slam, that of Jan Berry in the opening seconds. The duo later went on to host the Tami Show, a '60s. pop extravaganza featuring The Mama's and Papa's, The Who, The Rolling Stones, etc. Jan & Dean entered on skateboards and the link with youth culture was fixed.

Skateboarding was booming. *"Skater Dater"*, a Powell vid forerunner, won an Academy Award. The first pressure-moulded fibreglass board appeared courtesy of the Hobie label. G&S came out with a wood and plastic "fibreflex" board. Jan and Dean gave the "Little Old Lady" name to the first "sponsored" board and Life magazine and Newsweek covered the new "fad". Everything was on the up – sales, profits and injuries, **lots** of injuries. Metal and clay wheels jammed on the slightest contact with pebbles, hurling the rider to a certain slam. Pads were a later invention!

By Christmas '67, American shops were full of skateboards. **Fact:** no one bought them! Skating suffered a painful death which sent many companies to the wall. Why didn't people buy the boards? Well, the Beach Boys were growing fatter and the West Coast was full of flowers. Money went on Sgt Pepper albums, kaftans, beads, and many of the other indulgences of the time.

Well, that's one guess, anyway, but it's not necessarily the truth. Skateboarding is like politics, it goes in cycles – left-right-left-right, boom then bust. People are fickle and the youth aren't blind consumers. Yet as with politics, many cling to their allegiance through the unfashionable years. Many surf-skaters of the late '60s and early '70s discovered community fun in slalom, ditches, and backyard pools. The boards were limited, but they shredded and enjoyed. A California high had another meaning to them – blue tile carves. We're talking eleven feet!

The catalyst to the '70s craze that was skateboarding is one word. URETHANE. In 1973 Frank Nasworthy worked in conjunction with the Cadillac Wheel Company to convert their urethane trainer rollerskate wheels into a major breakthrough – the first wheel specifically designed for skateboards. This wheel had something special, grip traction! This expanded the skateboard's trick repertoire from simple hang tens, slalom, wheelies and carves to far more complicated and enthralling stunts. Further technical improvements in trucks, boards and bearings meant skateboarding took off worldwide at an alarming rate. Faster than green Kryps, even!

Four man catamaran
'70s style

The '70s, the skateboard "craze", major promotions, big time venues, TV and the "LA Run", Carlsbad and Anahiem skateparks, John Travolta, Jonny Rotten, tight shorts and white "Hang Ten" socks. Rainbow colour pads fail to prevent ROSPA outcries but ducks skateboard and so do presidents, prime ministers and heirs to the throne. Think heroes: Jay Adams, Mark Sinclair, Tony Alva, Mark Baker, Stacy Peralta. It just won't stop growing. Meanwhile one, Skate City, Marc Bolan Show, films, Leif Garrett, "Skateboard", "Skateboarder", bye-laws, **LAWS**! The progression to seemingly impossible tricks rages on – high-jump, 360's, 720's, 4 out blocks, wheelers, grinds, roll ins, roll outs and airs! Disco-fever changes to Punk rock pogoes and as the last safety pin plunges in, the bubble bursts. "Too much too young!"

Skateboarding grew so fast in the '70s that its death became not only inevitable, but also desirable. With such rapid progression, skateboarding needed time to take stock of all the new developments and seek to sustain itself through something more substantial than simple youth consumerism. Although 1979 heralded the official postmortem on '70s skateboarding, it had also seen some prophetic developments. By the start of 1979 the first ollie had been popped, into the media limelight, by Alan Gelfand. The first flat bottomed ramps had appeared, and every manufacturer had copied Dogtown and Alva with the "modern day" wide decks. Skaters talked of "ollie-airs" and Jay Smiths "laybacks". Parks closed but the foundations for the '80s were laid.

"Skateboarding went out with the bowler hat ... grow up!"

This was the common comment, but the years '79 to '85 gave birth to a worldwide skateboarding hardcore whose attitude and commitment may finally win skateboarders the same respect that their distant cousins, surfers, have achieved. This can only prevent the roller coaster of skateboard history taking another dip. Although technically the early '80s were tough times for skaters (facilities were few and far between, equipment was expensive and, let's face it, you were blatantly unfashionable), for many these were golden years. Skateboarding could not make you rich any more. You did it because you loved it and you knew those who skated with you did so for the same reason. Skateboarding was underground, skateboarders were the rebels.

Stacy Peralta in his formative years

Staggering early Ollie

Shogo Kubo

'80s hardcore, recessions, riots, Devo sounds and thrashing twangs, B52's, word of mouth comps and thriving fanzines, Reagan, Thatcher, Thrasher and Transworld, Bones Brigade Bombers on yellow T's, built to grind trucks for the hardcore only, California's Del Mar, Upland and Palmdale parks, Mile High and Clown ramps. London Skates Dominates! But Europe integrates. The south bank nights after Crystal Palace days – indys, mutes, japans, eggplants, beanplants. "The Future's Primitive" on a crackly pirate video, inverts, smiths, madonnas, money, gods! Grommets! Stickers!

These were golden years indeed, yet all the time skaters were asking, "When will we get respect?" "Is skateboarding going to be big again?" Perhaps some day skateboarders will be afforded the respect they deserve, for today skateboarding is bigger than ever. Skateboarding today is healthy and firmly in the black. Today it is not a "craze" but it could be more of a youth cult? Or a sport? An art? Attitude? Whatever it is, it's on what appears to be a steady course.

Competition is healthy, but not everything. Commercially, skateboarding is not so much a killing as an investment. Technically it is more diverse and interesting than ever before. '89's vert and street have opened a whole new range of possibilities which are by no means exhausted. The pro scene has meant advancement without exploitation, and new ramps and obstacles constantly amaze. Lessons from the past appear to have been learned. Skaters are finally beginning to take control. Things are on the up and up, and this time it's healthy cynicism that's keeping it that way.

Build metal ramps – prepare for the crash!

Danny Webster backside boneless,
Crystal Palace

"From each according to his abilities to each according to his needs."
Karl Marx.

Your first board will be unbelievably awful. You asked for the stars and you got the sewer. The wheels cone after two runs, the trucks turn then stay turned, the concave convexes. Friends laugh and take the mick. **Learn:** Mothers cannot buy skateboards! You love your board, though, and you'll keep it forever, for it is an education. To know what you like in a board and what set-up you prefer, it is necessary first to know what you *don't* like and why. First boards teach you this.

With 90% of the current equipment on the market the choice you have to make is not usually between good and bad, it's what you like and what you don't. It is obviously best to avoid boards that snap and trucks that crack but simple consumer advice should prevent such purchases. When you are thinking of investing in a new board you should always ask your friends, try their boards and seek their views. If you have no friends, ask the staff at any reputable skate store for advice, also try Clearasil, Gold Spot and an anti-dandruff shampoo. If the problem persists seek medical advice.

Decks The average deck these days is roughly about 10" by 30" and made of a seven ply lamination of hard rock maple with a deep concave and a steep tail. The deep concave gives a good foot placement, helping to keep the board in contact with the feet during assorted tricks. The width of the board has developed to give good stability when riding vertical terrain, and to incorporate company names over six letters! Thinner, more '70s-style boards are still available if you want to wimp out into slalom or freestyle. Epoxy laminate boards are also fairly common, and have the advantage of being lighter, although they are more prone to snapping, and are best for exclusive ramp usage.

The main consideration when buying any board, however, is obviously ... the graphics! People will not believe you can skate unless you have a variety of gross satanic imagery screen printed on your board. When in doubt always go for skull or pirate motifs, sure winners that are guaranteed to help you perform the most complicated tricks.

Trucks The purpose of the truck is two-fold. Firstly, it is an axle by which the wheels are connected to the board. Secondly, it is the skateboard's steering device. The majority of these trucks are made from heat treated aluminium, although combinations are becoming more popular, with weight saving plastic or nylon base plates being the most common example of this material exchange. Magnesium trucks are light and durable but also very expensive and usually the preserve of professional skaters. The widths of trucks vary between 8¾" (159s) to 9" (169s). These wider trucks are preferred for vert, bank, and street skating. Narrower trucks are more suitable for freestyle and slalom.

Advice on trucks is not hard to find. Trackers – "Tractors, mate!" Independents – "Undependents!" Gullwings – "Leadwings more like!" Heed **not** such pearls of wisdom! Pro skaters use most of the leading brands with few problems. You need trucks that turn and return, that survive the gnarly grinds but don't weigh a ton. When thinking of trucks don't ignore the rubbers. The heavier you are, the harder they'll need to be and the wrong rubbers can make a considerable difference. New trucks can look pretty lame but that authentic ground look can be achieved with simple glasspaper and elbow grease.

Wheels

All wheels today are manufactured from urethane compounds. These compounds come in varying hardnesses, specified by their "DUROMETER". The durometer of a wheel is given in a numerical way – the higher the number, the harder the wheel. The majority of wheels come in just three hardnesses: 97A, 95A, and 92A. 97A wheels are considered best for ramps, and 92A and 95A are good for street, although 97A is commonly used on the street as most skaters only possess one set. Back in the '70s, or "good old days" as they're commonly referred to, the size of wheels was around 65mm and above the thinking being that the bigger the wheel, the better the roll. Up until about 1987, 60mm was the norm in wheel size, but now 62mm and 66mm are more common. In truth wheel size has less to do with skating performance, and more to do with the fashions and whims of companies and consumers alike.

Roskopp pukes a slime ball

You'll find most skateboard wheels are now dual radius, fully reversible with centre set bearings to give even wear and prolong life. The width of wheels now averages between 36mm and 46mm. The narrow wheel lends itself to greater speed, but gives less traction. Some of the most popular wheels being made are by Santa Crus and Powell Peralta, and most these days are given names which resemble bands at the demented end of the heavy metal market. Always consider colour when buying wheels. If you don't complement your slide boards you could be making a serious fashion mistake. Also take notice of the common adage, "Pink wheels are for freestylers, and green wheels make you sterile."

Footwear The best footwear for skating should be grippy, hi-top, tough and flexible. You should be able to "feel" the board through the sole. Flat bottomed shoes hold a considerable advantage over the increasing number of heavy tread, cushion soled shoes that are on the market. Companies such as Vans, Airwalk, Hogs, and Vision all make specialist shoes with skaters in mind, considering things such as ollie and knee slide wear. Most manufacturers, Converse for instance, make their shoes in canvas, which is probably the best all round material for flexibility, durability, and price. Suede and leather boots are often as good if not better. It just seems that at the price you pay for them it's a shame to use them for skating!

Prolonging the life of your shoes can be done in a couple of ways. The application of shoe gum to your toe caps will help prevent ramp wear due to kneeslides and the quick use of "Duck Tape" (a sticky fabric insulation tape) can patch and protect any wearing, possibly halting rips before major holes appear.

Clothing Choosing what to wear, be it for every day or for skating, is a matter of personal taste. It should come naturally. If it doesn't, you are a clueless individual. The clueless individual is the consumer dream of the vast plethora of skate/surf clothing manufacturers. It is easy for the clueless individual to be cajoled then swamped in the costly, day-glow garb of leading brand names, ending up looking like the young fashion victim in a soap powder commercial. Think for youself! It does help!

Whatever you choose, be it the West Coast excesses of Christian Hosoi, the homeboy blatantness of Steve Cab or the barrow boy style of Bill Danforth, the bottom line is anything you wear must serve a simple function – you must be able to skate in it. Long shorts, beefy T's and lose sweats are all ideal for skating. The rest is your choice, but remember, whatever you wear it's going to get trashed!

Grova rocks "The Limelight"

Fashion victim

"Seek and ye shall find."
St Matthew 7.

TERRAIN

Where to skate is not a problem. Having nowhere to skate is an excuse not a reality. Claustrophobia (the morbid dread of enclosed spaces) plagues many skaters. It locks you into conformity. **The key?** Never to take reality as the sum of your knowledge. **The cure?** Seeking, searching, shredding terrain. In every twentieth century settlement, no matter what its size, there is skating terrain. Whether it's a carpark or a kerb, there's always something. The skateboard evolved for urban living yet even in the wilderness, if imagination and the ability to construct exist, so can skateboarding. Most, however, do not live in the wilderness (if indeed it's still there) and have other considerations when choosing terrain. Snake sessions with pedestrians in a mall or cars on the road can prove fun, but also fatal and both are best avoided. Where to skate is not a problem, what to skate can be, and making choices always is.

Parks Probably the most obvious place to skate is a skatepark – a custom built arena for the use of skaters. Today these are few and far between and often built in a time when lip was just something you gave your parents. In a decent park you should find many concrete delights: snake runs, pipes, combi pools, bowls, moguls, and other skateable (and not so skateable) terrain. The age of many of these parks often means the inclusion of unique follies designed by a non-skating, clueless council or corporate employee. Amazingly tight snake runs, banks with gravel bottoms and assorted concrete sculptures will no doubt confuse any future historian on a post apocalypse field trip.

Most parks (paying and non-paying) now have a ramp to skate as well, and some parks are now ramp only. It is the concrete, though, that can provide unique days and memories. Snaking is seldom a problem in such rolling places and skaters of varying abilities can all find somewhere to skate and something to do. For the novice, skateparks are a definite recommendation. They'll help you to find your feet and progress without the seemingly unattainable challenge of vert, or the trick facism of the street. In parks "flow and style" can be learned and improved, something from which all aspects of your skating will benefit.

For a time parks were just dozed, not built but, while the last few years have seen the loss of some of the great parks (Upland and Del Mar in the U.S. and Gillingham in the U.K.), new ones are being built. There are state-of-the-art indoor parks in Sminge and Milwaukee, both incorporating concrete pools of the keyhole and clover leaf type.

The Pipeline, Upland

Carlsbad Skatepark,
California

At the now defunct Del
Mar, Carlsbad

Brent Fellows: Frontside Air, Swansea

Ramps

Ramps **are** modern skateboarding, having been instrumental in the progression of the sport. The basic flat bottomed half-pipe construction is now evolving into a sculptural challenge. From tomb stones to escalators, through minis and W7s to full scale bowls, ramps are providing some of the most challenging terrain available. Mini ramps are a good place to learn your basics, try new tricks, and improve your style. They are also at the forefront of ramp design. Their size and relatively easy construction has enabled a good deal of experimentation to take place in dimensions and surfaces, and this has been passed on to their bigger brothers. This means that it is now very hard to say what an average half-pipe is. The emphasis is on variation. Should it be wood, metal, masonite, or plexy glass? Should it have 2ft or 1½ft of vert? A channel or tombstone? The truth is, ramps, like skaters, should be and are individuals.

Craig Johnson; Handplant, Southsea

Skatepark of Houston Texas

ools The drained swimming pool is the classic terrain. It has always been at the soul of the cultivated romantic fantasy that has permeated the skating scene. Pools provided the first vertical terrain, and the basic grinds, airs and handplants which form the bulk of today's ramp tricks were all developed in drained pools. The popularity of pools meant that many skateparks incorporated pools in their design, including the compulsory blue tiles.

Pools are usually transient terrain. Swimming pools, be they private or public, have the annoying habit of being filled with water 90% of the year, and if you're lucky enough to find an empty one it is rare that it's both transitional and available to skate. For this reason most skateable pools are usually deserted ones, nestling in the backyard of some burnt-out household or lying drained and dormant behind some deadbeat motel. Even with deserted pools, the tresspass laws ensure that most are mortal – with but a short summer to live.

This has meant that some of the most popular pools which have lasted the years are in the middle of nowhere. They may take a full scale expedition to find (eg Bastrop in Texas, The Nude Bowl in Arizona and Neasden in London) but you are usually rewarded with a classic day. Pools come in many shapes: square, kidney, keyhole, etc, but all require a certain style, speed, and ability. Pools are carved and worked, the line being essential. Certain pools do lend themselves to tricks but pool skating is in essence a pure form of skating and ultimately one of the most rewarding.

Neasden

Will

Jason Florio

Mark Baker hitches a ride

Street The terms "street" and "street style" are used to label a variety of what are best described as obstacles, some of which occur naturally and some of which do not. All are available to those who search. Pavements, kerbs, benches, bollards, parking blocks, hand rails and walls are all readily available to your average punter. Coping, slidebars, jump ramps, pyramid ramps, etc. are, on the other hand, **not** omnipresent by everybody's door, unless they've constructed and put them there or they happen to live in some unheard of paradise. So, when hearing of street skate comps, do not confuse this with the skating of the street.

The skating of the street is one of the more common enjoyments in terrain. It enables the skateboard to be transportation. The ollie has become **the** street trick, for without it transportation is not fluent and is broken by kerbs and cracks. Street skating is, by its nature, a public event and tricks develop a sense of open exhibitionism (how else can you explain frontside hand rail slides?). This public presence often means public pressure. In theory you have as much right to skate the street as you do to push a shopping trolley down it or roll your wheelchair up it. In practice you are open to a great deal of public prejudices and pettiness.

Skateboarding is a crime in many states and countries, but if you can happily morally justify your skating, then by all means do so. Exposing contradictions and hypocrisy is best done by direct action, although conflict and martyrdom is, at best, naive. Street skating is about fun, obviously, but it is constricted terrain and usually limited to just that – fun. For a more complete skate, try the street at night. It's a different place, with few of the day's more pedestrian problems!

Shane O'Brien – Kingston

Cabellero – South Bank

Lance Mountain

Ditches,
Drains
and Pipes Human history is heavy with the desire to control nature. Water is an essential element for human survival and through the ages mankind (and womankind!) has sought to control this vital resource. Floods are not a wholly desirable phenomenon and the 20th century concrete culture enabled water to be channelled, if not mastered, hence the construction of ditches, drains and pipes.

Skating history is heavy with the desire to control the concrete. Concrete is an essential element for skateboarding's survival and through the years skaters have sought to control this vital resource.

Skating ditches etc. can satisfy nearly all of a skater's desires. Like the search for pools, it caters for the explorer and soul searcher as well as the carver and shredder. To speed freaks, if skating has a saint its shrine is in California where Mt Baldy, The Line and The Pipe are perhaps the ultimate. Texas ditches are a scene and style of their own – Whip and Dip, EZ7 and Slaughter Lane. If ramps are the heart and pools the soul, then ditches, drains and pipes are the spirit.

FFEJ – Nollie boardslide

Natas – Fire hydrant Ollie

Mark Gonzales

Architectural Skatespots Although modern architecture has its critics, few of them skate. The myriad of "carbuncles" that have infested our cities inadvertently blessed the skating populace with an abundance of skating amentities. This terrain, be it Gothic, Deco, Bauhaus, Modernist, or Post Modernist, can contain features that demand skaters' attention. You can debate their aesthetic qualities but sights such as London's South Bank Centre make you appreciate the architect's ability to create irresistible skating areas. It appears that nearly every town has its own office block, shopping precinct, or police station with its own set of banks. The true delight of such architectural features is in their diversity. Marble, brick and concrete are all sloping somewhere along with grindable lips and transitions to 30ft of vert. Structural diversity, not uniformity, has proved to be modernism's strength as far as skaters are concerned.

Sculptures, parklands, and other civic ornamentations are also a source of terrain but did the sculptor of Lenin's statue in Prague consider its plinth with grinds in mind? Did the artist behind the Fish Banks in California envisage fakie cess slides? It's doubtful, yet few would object to such combinations of creativity. Skateboarding is an urban pursuit. In skating architecture you are tackling your urban environment. By doing this you mentally control its threatening excesses and high rise horrors become tame. Where current post modernism and neo classicism are failing to provide the terrain that modernism achieved, hopefully forthcoming movements will hold the "incline" and "transition" essential to their manifestos.

E. Dressen – Ollie to table

Danny Webster: Crystal Palace

Steve Wiltshire, Texas Plant

J. Boy – Sweeper

Jeff Grosso, Tailslide

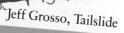

Kevin Stabb, Frontside Smith

Ken Park – One-footed Eggplant

Jean-Marc Vaisette – Footbreaker

"Either he's dead or his watch has stopped."
Groucho Marx.

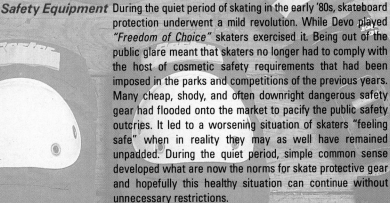

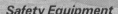

Skateboarding is not a safe pursuit, neither is cycling, horse racing, or skiing. You do not skateboard under the pretence that it is safe – a high wire act is not exciting one foot off the ground. The danger is often the excitement and the spur. You **will** get hurt skateboarding but the trick is to limit any damage you may receive to the simple wear and tear of cuts and bruises that do not hamper your enjoyment. Simple safety precautions can mean the difference between a scabby elbow and a broken arm. Ignoring safety is not hardcore, it's just naive.

Safety Equipment

During the quiet period of skating in the early '80s, skateboard protection underwent a mild revolution. While Devo played *"Freedom of Choice"* skaters exercised it. Being out of the public glare meant that skaters no longer had to comply with the host of cosmetic safety requirements that had been imposed in the parks and competitions of the previous years. Many cheap, shody, and often downright dangerous safety gear had flooded onto the market to pacify the public safety outcries. It led to a worsening situation of skaters "feeling safe" when in reality they may as well have remained unpadded. During the quiet period, simple common sense developed what are now the norms for skate protective gear and hopefully this healthy situation can continue without unnecessary restrictions.

If you are going to skate vert, pipes, pools, mini ramps, etc you'll need some sort of protection. When skating vert it is advisable to wear a helmet, elbow and knee pads, and if you choose hip pads, wrist guards and gloves this should provide you with all the protection you need, whilst still enabling you to skate.

Helmets should be lightweight but strong, "fly-aways" and "protecs" (highly recommended) are essential for ramp wear, head injury being probably the worst injury you could receive. Elbow and knee pads by either Rector or Pro Design **will** protect you. They are expensive (especially custom-made Pro Designs) but are designed for and by skaters and imitations are not the same.

Always make sure your pads are on tightly and that the straps are secure, as wearing loose pads can create worse injuries. Wrist guards are a good idea, as this is one of your body's weakest points. Many people say they find them awkward and that they just shuttle any potential break further up your arm. There may be an element of truth in this, but 90% of the time you will not break your arm instead of your wrist. Your arm is a lot less fragile than your wrist and should the worst come to the worst your arm is far more easily repaired. As for wrist guards being "awkward", it is just a question of getting used to them and if you start skating with them you will feel awkward **without** them. Wrist guards are also the most practical form of protection for the street other than gloves.

Gloves provide good protection for all types of skating. They prevent your hands contacting all the glass, splinters and grit which cause big slams. When skating mini ramps, banks, or street, you will probably require less protection. This protection should always be weighed against practicality and your own limitations. A helmet can impair vision in street skating, and as head injuries are rare on the street, the wearing of one can actually be unsafe. On the other hand, knee pads will do you no harm, although they can prevent manoeuvrability making them probably only advisable for beginners. You will soon find your personal protection needs and any weak area of your body that needs special attention. Above all, never underestimate potential slams and know your limitations.

Joe Evans, meanwhile two

Bailing Learning to fall is the only way you're going to be able to learn to stay on. Bailing correctly should prevent any major injury, and is well worth learning.

Slam Avoidance Apart from deliberate bails, slams are usually the result of either a failure in equipment, a dodgy surface, or a collision. It is always wise to check the following when skating.

1. That your equipment is in full working order. Loose nuts and small cracks have a nasty habit of falling off or splitting at a moment's notice.
2. That of the ramp, park, pool or sidewalk you're skating on has no broken glass or loose pebble ornamentation.
3. That the way is clear, the view is long, and your eyes are tested regularly!

Lance Mountain – layed back bail

Street Bailing street tricks is best avoided. Usually it will be quite easy just to jump off your board at any moments of apprehension. When travelling at speed just jumping off can lead to several problems. The advice is to keep low (not so far to fall), roll with your motion (cuts your speed gradually) and relax, (preventing breakages). How you're supposed to do all this (especially relax) is another matter, but the advice **is** sound. The best way, however, is to make sure you're not travelling out of control at a speed where this advice is needed!

Ramps The most common move in all ramp skating is not the kick turn but the knee slide. All knee pads today are designed for this specific act. Basically it is a way out of trouble. If you're at the top of a ramp and something goes wrong, be it a hang up or whatever, first throw your board away (or distance yourself from it any way you can) then twist or redefine your body into "bail position".

This involves tucking your legs under you, facing towards the ramp bottom and sliding with the weight on your knee pads. This can be practised by throwing yourself off the top of a ramp or (probably more sensibly) running up the transition and jumping, then twisting. The correct way to learn is from a fellow skater, not a book, and once learned it will become an automatic life saver.

Preparing to bail

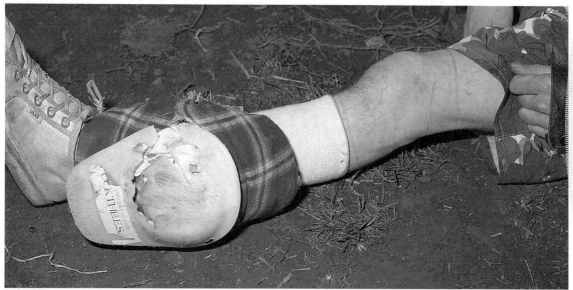

Gnarled knee

Basic Treatments If you find you have any major complaints, clicking knees etc. always seek proper medical attention, but for most everyday injuries simple first aid rules will suffice. Small cuts and grazes are best left alone. Simply disinfect with an antiseptic cream then leave (until they get "crispy" when picking can be fun). Bruises can be brought up by the application of witch hazel, which will also help your immediate circulation. Knees can be kept in good condition by regular massage with a compound liniment. Wearing neoprene gaskets or "Smith Skins" under your knee pads will help give your knees support as well as keeping them at a steady temperature – thus helping to prevent torn ligaments. Your body can be kept in general good shape by the application of a mixture of baby and lavender oils. This will make your body supple and increase blood circulation, both of which help heal skate injuries or prevent long term effects. This treatment also has the benefit of making you smell nice – one thing that *few* skaters achieve.

Imminent disaster

When to call an ambulance Some slams are worse than others and on those occasions when someone is hurt, the simple guideline is to ask the injured person if they need an ambulance. Their body will tell them when this is necessary! If by any chance they don't answer at all, call help immediately. Don't move them, keep them warm, breathing and prevent any blood flow. If limbs are spread about, gather them up to give to the doctor on arrival.

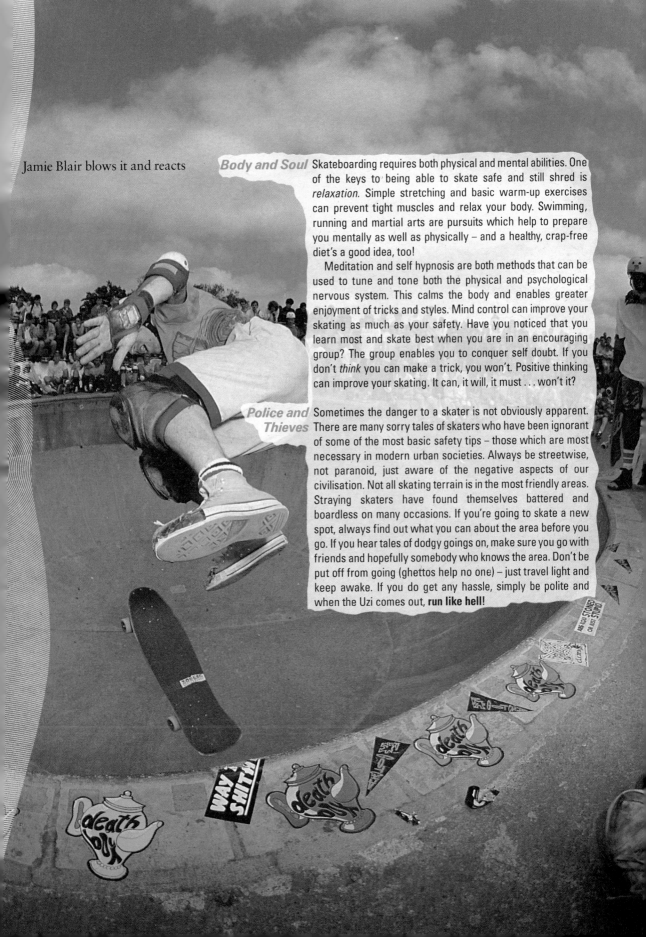

Jamie Blair blows it and reacts

Body and Soul Skateboarding requires both physical and mental abilities. One of the keys to being able to skate safe and still shred is *relaxation*. Simple stretching and basic warm-up exercises can prevent tight muscles and relax your body. Swimming, running and martial arts are pursuits which help to prepare you mentally as well as physically – and a healthy, crap-free diet's a good idea, too!

Meditation and self hypnosis are both methods that can be used to tune and tone both the physical and psychological nervous system. This calms the body and enables greater enjoyment of tricks and styles. Mind control can improve your skating as much as your safety. Have you noticed that you learn most and skate best when you are in an encouraging group? The group enables you to conquer self doubt. If you don't *think* you can make a trick, you won't. Positive thinking can improve your skating. It can, it will, it must . . . won't it?

Police and Thieves Sometimes the danger to a skater is not obviously apparent. There are many sorry tales of skaters who have been ignorant of some of the most basic safety tips – those which are most necessary in modern urban societies. Always be streetwise, not paranoid, just aware of the negative aspects of our civilisation. Not all skating terrain is in the most friendly areas. Straying skaters have found themselves battered and boardless on many occasions. If you're going to skate a new spot, always find out what you can about the area before you go. If you hear tales of dodgy goings on, make sure you go with friends and hopefully somebody who knows the area. Don't be put off from going (ghettos help no one) – just travel light and keep awake. If you do get any hassle, simply be polite and when the Uzi comes out, **run like hell!**

"Curiouser and curiouser!" cried Alice.
Alice in Wonderland, Lewis Carroll.

Don Brown: top English freestyler

'DIFFERENT STROKES FOR DIFFERENT FOLKS'

Skateboarding is currently dominated by both street skating and ramp. Subsequently these are what most skaters indulge in. There are, however, many other aspects of skateboarding which, although not as popular, are supported with equal enthusiasm. Many of these variations are legacies from the '70s, others are mutations on a theme but all provide variety.

Freestyle Freestyle has been around since the '60s, and although 360's and Hang Tens are now anathema to most freestylers, such terms and imagery still fuel the perceptions of non-freestyling skaters and the general public alike. Freestyle today could best be described as street skating without the obstacles – a series of tricks performed on the flat and usually in a routine. At its best, freestyle is inventive, intricate, skilful and exciting. At worst it is grown men in tight shorts and white socks performing the skateboard equivalent of some pretentious ice dance.

Freestyle is one of the most competitive aspects of skateboarding, and along with slalom it is the closest to clearcut "sport" that skateboarding comes. The only time you actually see more than one freestyler in any one place, there is usually a competition going on. In competition they will have practised a set routine and usually semi-synchronised it to a chosen music track. They'll perform two or more runs and be judged accordingly. Freestyle comps are pretty much international affairs with skaters like Pierre Andre, Per Wilender, Don Brown, Shane Rouse, and Hans Lindgren constantly sparring with each other.

While freestyle tends to be a rather insular world, certain individuals stand out. The obvious is Rodney Mulen whose skill, style, and technique is appreciated by all skateboarders.

The freestyle scene is permanently threatening to expand, yet the problem appears to be that most younger skaters can only afford one board and are buying street/ramp boards rather than the more limiting freestyle board. The freestyle board is smaller and thinner than a ramp board, with less of a kicktail. It's almost totally unsuitable for anything except freestyle moves.

The future for freestyle may lie in street skating. YoYo Schultz's handy trademark has been incorporated into street skating for many years now, and other more applicable moves are now creeping in. This crossover of freestyle into street skating is one of the more interesting recent developments in skateboarding and, although freestyle in its more traditional form will not die, the future probably lies in the crossover.

Rodney Mullen S.F.

Slalom Slalom is another of the more traditional skating activities. It's thought these days to be the preserve of a few misguided weirdos – and on the whole it is. It doesn't get much coverage but is still strong enough (mainly in Europe) to justify several annual competitions and the rather groovey quarterly fanzine "Slalom!"

Slalom boards have fat, high traction wheels (usually Kryps), loose, easy turn trucks and thin boards with camber and flex. This helps enable an easy passage through the cones. The way in which the cones are set up dictates the type of slalom event. Parallel slalom is when the cones are set out in a straight line at a set distance from each other, usually with another similar line parallel to them. Skaters compete on a head to head basis, often from a ski-style ramp start. Cones can be staggered in semi-abstract patterns, which requires more agility and less reliance on speed.

Races are timed with penalties for missing or knocking over cones. Often giant slalom courses are set up on long downhill stretches and here the comparison with slalom skiing is at its most obvious. These days the main thing slalom skaters appear to have in common is that they drink – these guys *really* drink. To be able to down 7 or 8 pints of beer is a must in the slalom world and 11-12 is more appropriate! Maybe this is why they prefer skating in wavey lines!

"No but seriously!" Edwin

Downhill Racers: Brands Hatch

Downhill While many still enjoy the downhill thrills and have done since the days of La Costa, the serious downhill skate community is small but passionate. Speed is the essential word in downhill and is obtained through equipment and style.

Skaters use long decks with up to eight wheels, some with streamlined fairings. For ultimate speed they employ the "luge" style, dressed in a one-piece, skin-tight suit, with an aerodynamic helmet. After crouching forward first for speed they lie on their backs, arms gripping the sides, heads peering up occasionally to check direction. In this style Roger Hickey (Mr Downhill) recently took the speed record to 78mph and confirmed his place in the Guinness Book of Records. Good old Roger.

The average downhill is not so much racing as dorking. Witness some of the terrifying descents seen in the Powell videos where skaters crouch on their boards, checking their speed via lay back slides, their hands protected by palm pad gloves. With such gloves, hard wheels, tight trucks, and nerves of steel, speeding down a steep road can be the purest fun on the skateboard, providing you don't meet a truck coming the other way!

One man and his dog

High Jump A lot of people think high jump died along with that other skating curiosity, barrel jumping. It may as well have, but it is still practised (mainly in Eastern Europe and the Soviet Union) and warrants a mention.

Basically the skaters ride along on a 3-4ft board/plank, jumping off over a bar and landing back on the moving board. The height is measured not from the ground but from the top of the deck thus preventing the use of 6ft riser pads! The current world record of 5ft 7in was set by Trevor Baxter in 1982. A high jump competition can be very entertaining to watch and is by its nature climactic, something which may keep it alive even though the minority who pursue it are becoming more minor each year.

Snowboarding Snowboarding has finally come of age. It's no longer a mixture of surfing, skiing and skateboarding but an entity in its own right. Snowboarding, though, is still basically skateboarding on snow, and the tricks, the halfpipes, and the attitude all bear this out.

Snowboards, like decks, come in varying shapes and sizes, you pays your money you takes your chances, but Burton and Sims both have an established reputation. Bindings and boots are now being specially made for snowboards, although standard ski equipment is easily adapted. Many skateboarders have now taken to spending their winters snowboarding. This has been encouraged by the snowboarders themselves who are trying to prevent the onslaught of attention by skiing's yuppie element. Snowboarding is expanding all the time and with high skater involvement, it should develop into a healthy winter alternative.

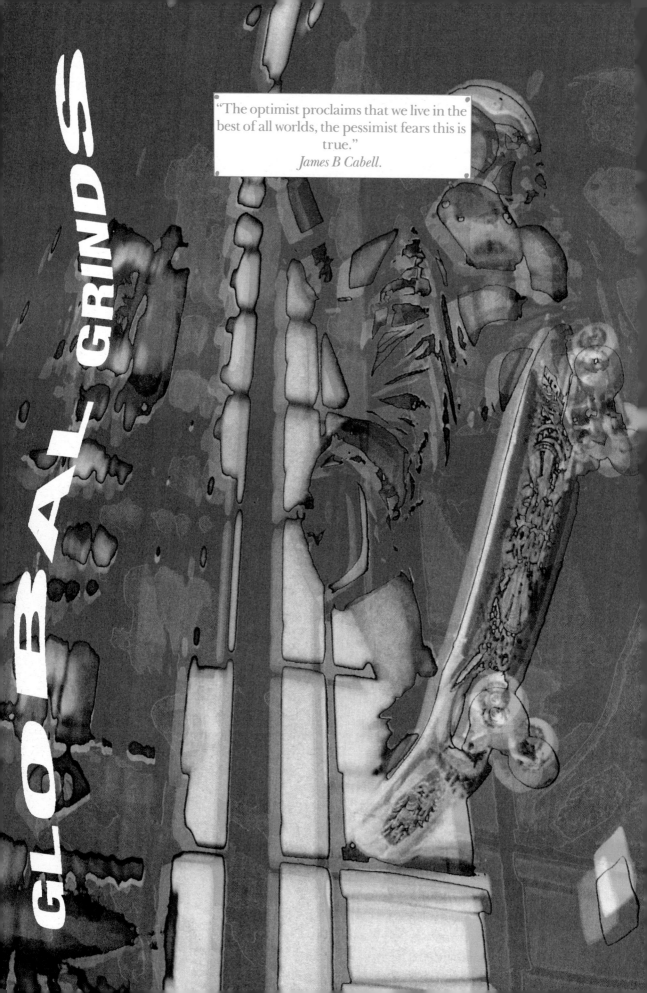

GLOBAL GRINDS

"The optimist proclaims that we live in the best of all worlds, the pessimist fears this is true."
James B Cabell.

Don Brider and friends: France

Skateboarding is a global pursuit. Most countries that are not ravaged by wars, famine, disaster, and disease have a skate community of one sort or another. While the bulk of skateboard equipment and pro's continue to come from the United States, America no longer enjoys the world domination that it once had. Styles and priorities vary from country to country and even town to town but the skateboarding attitude appears to run along a universal thread and on many levels. There is little to differentiate between skaters in Milwaukee and those in Moscow.

The global aspect of the skateboarding scene can be very rewarding for those who are willing and able to travel. Many skaters spend their vacations travelling around America, Europe, Australia, and beyond. They session local spots, sightsee and often end up sleeping on floors in the homes of other skaters they've met. Cheap travel with helpful local guides has an obvious appeal and many people swap international addresses with the same zeal some show for stickers.

The Skating World In Europe skating is at its most popular in Germany, United Kingdom, Holland and Scandinavia, but there is a significant scene in practically all European countries (East and West). There is a wide diversity of skate facilities in Europe with first class skateparks in Madrid (Spain) and Livingstone in Scotland. Numerous others exist in England, Denmark, Holland, and Germany. Ramps are appearing at a steady rate with Britain now boasting over 30 including two of the world's finest, Swansea and Latimer Road. The leading European manufacturers are 'Death Box' (UK) and 'Titus' (GDR) both of whom have their own products, teams, and sponsorship deals.

Many Euro pro's such as Bod Boyle (UK), Claus Grabke (GDR), Nicky Guerrero (DEN), Hans Lindgren (SWE) and Tony Magnussen (SWE) are often mistaken for Americans. This is because the top stars find the facilities and financial rewards (as well as the Californian weather!) so much better in America, but that could change as other nations start to fly the skateboard flag. Some of the biggest skateboard scenes outside Europe and North America are in Australia and Brazil, both scenes stemming from their vibrant beach culture.

Claus Grabke, Munster

Barry Abrook: stylish tail grab smith grind

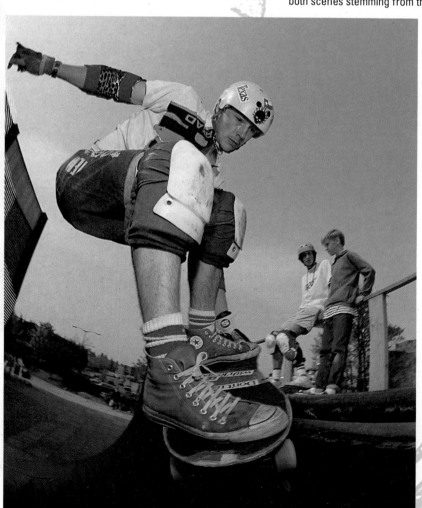

Australia boasts ramps, shops and magazines which spread its scene as far as Bali and New Zealand, well established surfer haunts. Few pro's dominate down under but names such as Grego Rankine (NZ/AUS) and Lee Ralph (NZ) confirm the area's high standard.

Brazil's scene is particularly off the wall. The country which has an awful lot of coffee also has an awful lot of counterfeiting. Most of the items of equipment used by Brazilian skaters are counterfeit copies of American goods. Fake Santa Cruz decks, fake Indy's, fake OJ's, and numerous fake Vans. This, usually appallingly bad, equipment is widespread but relied upon for economic reasons and it is a tribute to Brazilian skaters that they can not only stay on such dodgy equipment but shred as well.

Japan had a skatepark at Chiba as early as 1976, and since then skateboarding has always had a wide following although it is only recently that world rate pro's have appeared. Japan is also attracting American pro's over for comps and demo's, most of whom seem to be enjoying the experience.

Iceland, Czechoslovakia, Argentina, Nicaragua you name it, they all have skating facilities and skaters who use them. It shouldn't surprise you, once you understand that skateboarding is international and not confined to any one country or area. Travel broadens the mind. It helps skating and skateboarders develop an international feel for things. "World Cups" of one sort or another have become less sporadic occurrences, and it is refreshing to see that most skaters enter firstly on behalf of themselves, not as representatives of a country. There are no flag ceremonies or marching tracksuits. The cynics would say that this is because in a true international competition, America would wipe the board.

It's encouraging to think, however, that skateboarding crosses national and racial boundaries, making skaters one big, smiling, happy family. Do you remember those Coke adverts where they all hold hands and sing about the world? Well, like that! Next time you're stranded in Bilbao and your board's been stolen, along with passport, flight tickets, and Dad's "emergency only" credit card, just sing "I'd like to teach the world to skate ..." All your problems will just flow away and your mind will come to rest in a global grind. Sure it will . . . . .

Smileon: Skating in a Soviet stylee

FFEJ, German invert

"Our discussion is of no trifling matter, but on the right way to conduct our lives."
Plato, Republic VIII
. . . or . . .
"You don't need to watch Dynasty to have an attitude."
Kiss, Prince.

Salba and Phillips play Little and Large

Life's a pavement. Sometimes it goes uphill and sometimes it goes down. Sometimes it's as smooth as tarmacadam and sometimes it's like gravel. Occasionally you slip on something nasty, yet from beginning to end everyone is by their nature, pedestrian. Travelling on a skateboard, you rise above and overtake the pedestrian. Understand – skateboarding is the catalyst by which many rise above the pedestrian.

Multi Media Skateboarding supports a vast amount of magazines and videos, 90% of which (surprisingly enough) support and promote skaters as best they can. The pages of such established mags as "Transworld", "Thrasher" (US), and "Read and Destroy" (UK) now have many contemporaries including "Power Edge" (US), "Homeboy" (US), "Skateboard" (UK), "540" (AUS) and "Monster" (GDR), all of which are capable of providing a good read.

The video market is swamped with manufacturers' videos which promote their teams and products. Many of them are highly innovative, such as Gullwing & Vision, and some, like the Powell videos, "Future Primitive" and "Public Domain", have inspired many non-skate productions.

The best skate media, however, is the fanzine. Numerous photocopied slag rags blossom and wither at an alarming rate. Each captures a local scene and a moment in time. Few are readable, yet all are a tribute to skaters' creativity and classics like "Sketchy" zine are as much a part of skate history as "Thrasher".

Attitude Attitude is the great skate cliché – you've got to have it. Some people, no matter how well they skate, never become "skaters" because their attitude is wrong. Others pop a few ollies and are there straight away simply because they have the right attitude. Attitude separates Gods from grommets and skaters from society. To define such a variable is hard, yet it is, at its purest, the visable external sign of an uncorrupted soul.

Santacruz Skate Betty

Cheap Skating Skateboarding need not be expensive. Many trade shops sell secondhand goods at reasonable prices. A cheap standard graphicless deck is easily obtained at low cost and can be more than adequate. It is possible in theory to make any skate goods you need but it's highly debatable whether pouring your own wheels and forging your trucks would save you money! Good quality gear can be obtained at a reasonable price from pro's who are usually more than willing to sell it. Above all, don't take shop costs at face value. Secondhand goods can often provide some amazing deals when you consider extras like slide rails, griptape, etc.

Lucero dorks it up

Haircuts from Hell Skaters' haircuts have gone through many transitions from the flowing "Partridge Family" style locks of fake West Coast surfdom, to the shorn skulls of Bill Danforth clones. It appears that the first thing any pro does after he gets his board is to get a ridiculous haircut. How can anyone forget such classics as the Stacy wedge, the Bod crew, the Zorlac dreads, Florian Bohms "Marie Antoinette" style, and the jet black "wiggy" of Screaming Lord Salba?

Illusions in the crowd

Pro's Many skaters dream of pro'dem. The idea that you can skate all day and make money doing it is obviously appealing. In reality there are only a small number of pro's on this planet who actually make a decent living from skateboarding. The rest get by on product handouts, appearance fees, and occasional prize money. They don't complain (much) – it's the life they choose. The big money (as always) is in the hands of the manufacturers and retailers, more and more of which are being taken over by skaters who give something back to the movement.

To many, however, pro's are there just to hand out stickers, but a heart beats under that flashy promo T-shirt. The assumption by many a pleb that pro's are there to give away boards, trucks etc. can often gnaw right into the pro's soul. When he realises that the pleb demanding such benevolence is bedecked in the finest attire and probably has a nice bed to sleep in that night, he thinks of himself. Nine times out of ten the pro has to bum a lift from somebody to the next comp, then sleep on the floor of some obliging individual's less than sanitary house. Such is life at the top, give a pro a break!

Second Person Plural The problems with officialdom have been the same throughout skateboarding's ups and downs over the years. Official attitudes are somewhat bewildering. On one hand, they'll help build a park or ramp, but on the other, they'll ban skating from everywhere else. The truth is, the authorities in general do not understand skateboarding or skateboarders, and what they don't understand they attempt to suppress using any public safety nuisance excuse they can. The reality is that skateboarding is no more risky than canoeing, nor a bigger nuisance than shopping trolleys.

This ignorance towards skateboarding has become generally expected by skaters, and it's one area where the magazines and manufacturers should take a lead. Many do, yet some still choose to exploit rather than invest, which in crude business terms is not in their best interest. Greater and more sustained popularity will mean greater profits for them in the long term. Perhaps we should take a close look at the emerging scene in Eastern Europe where they invest in and promote skating, although incorporating it into some rather dubious sporting propaganda philosophies.

Barry Abrook
eggplant, Warrington

First Person Singular Ultimately, skating must be for yourself and other skaters, in effect a permanent glimpse of your future. Knowing this, the urge to control motion, defy gravity and overcome personal mental barriers becomes stronger. To advance to a level of trick creation is to have mastered an alternative art form, not an alternative sport.

irlies Traditionally, skateboarding has been rather a male dominated affair. "Bettys" were just a hindrance or a bit of fun. Now we live in liberated times and more females are appearing on the scene, many with a damn sight more bottle than their male counterparts. There are now sponsored female skaters in most skate disciplines and it should be hoped that they will soon become the norm rather than a novelty.

Sue Hazel, Farnborough comp

Ros Mertz, method lien

Easy Riders The essence of skating must be its freedom – a PURE rush, hurtling down a deserted pavement, cruising and ollieing the occasional drainage cover or kerb. It's a state of complete concentration, mind oblivious to the outside world. This is the essence of the biker world of "Easy Rider", an outlaw image combined with a Bohemian view of society. The philosophy was born from surf inspiration and '70s skating and it's still the ideal to which many adhere. First contacts with skating, and the subsequent nostalgia, ensure that thousands of skaters stay true to this attitude and resist straying into the more aggressive arena of the vertical.

Raw Power '80s skating can require an '80s attitude, kill or be killed, do or die. The hardcore of thrash imagery is a mind into motion "Go for it!" commitment. High airs and complex lip tricks almost require an inner self destruct mechanism. Once knowledge of basic moves is gained, the only thing between you and an easy passage to the gods is the indefinable "natural" ability combined with fearlessness and a good dose of luck. Few are blessed, and this is where aggression takes over, either naturally or forcedly. It's hard for any skater to have a complete disregard for their own well being, so replacing fear with aggression can relax your mind. A relaxed mind and an aggressive body is one proven formula for advancing your skating and forms the main push behind today's skate achievements.

Neither of these two states of mind should be taken as definitive. Like everything, skating is a progression, constantly revising and re-defining. The words "style" and "tricksey" can define decade differences, but combinations of both notions are always evident. Skating was never designed to be judged: there are too many conflicting ideas involved. Some skaters make difficult tricks constantly without fail, almost robot-like, soon becoming technically brilliant but "boring" to the onlooker. Stylish skaters, on the other hand, give onlookers the feel of past progression and the sense that there is more than just a trick going on. The same goes for the sketchy skaters. Even on the brink of disaster they force the onlooker to watch them, dragging their mind to devillish thoughts of impending doom. Gripping stuff, no matter which way you grab it!

Clowning around

Future Primitive? However long you've been skating and how well clued in you are is more or less irrelevant. The fact that skating is now so popular means a whole new generation, many of whom weren't even born in the '70s, can experience skating for the first time. There is now a myriad of layers that permeate skating, perpetuate its myths, breed new ones and either prevent or predict its downfall. Skating is different things to different people. The future may be miniramps, bowls, or W's but it sure won't be the same. Tolerance and respect for the differences have fuelled progressions in the same way the hardcore has. **NOT** being understood is not a problem, it's a plus. If an asylum is the norm, then being different is sanity. Don't fight it, enjoy it. Keep the faith.

Tommy Guerreo, Southsea

Layed Back: Devo-Tee

The building of skateboard ramps is constantly developing and being refined. There is, as such, no definite way of building a ramp, although most are built using the same basic methods of construction. The most common and easy to build has a timber frame and plywood surface. The following diagrams illustrate some of the basic principles needed to build such a structure. Before you begin building, try researching methods of construction from other ramps. Every ramp builder has his own way of constructing his ramp. Look for effective ways to cut costs and beef up your construction.

We have shown one way of fitting coping but you may want real pool coping of pvc tubing. You may also have access to building a full steel framed ramp, considered by some to be the ultimate in terms of strength and durability. One thing is for sure, once you understand the basic construction principles shown, you will be able to build jump ramp, slalom race start ramps, minis, full size contest ramps or a simple quarter pipe to prop up against a wall.

Decide what sort of ramp you want to build. What sort of radius you want your ramp to have? How high, how wide? Knowing this can only come with experience of riding other ramps. If your space and cash is limited you could do a lot worse than start with a mini ramp (see drawings). For a first time ramp builder there are many advantages to a mini ramp. For a start they use about one-third less wood than a full size ramp, they take up less room, make less noise (sometimes a problem in residential areas). However, if you've got the chance don't be afraid of building up to full size.

A good basic size for a mini or fun ramp might be sixteen feet wide, eight ½ foot transitions, five feet high with 12 feet of flat bottom. For a full size ramp try 24 feet wide 9 foot transitions with 1½ft of vertical, and 16 feet of flat bottom. This is only a suggestion, obviously you will be limited by space, money and personal preference. Try using your imagination, particularly with mini ramps. There are plenty of magazines and videos with interesting examples of some of the possibilities for ramp construction.

A well-built ramp can last several years with only the occasional resurfacing. A badly built ramp could become useless after an afternoon's skating. If you don't have the right equipment when you want to start building, wait! Spend an extra few weeks to make sure you have just enough bolts, screws, nails and especially wood to make your ramp really strong. Make sure that your crossbeams are not spaced too far apart, particularly on the lower portion of the transition. These provide the foundation of your riding surface. The more solid this is, the better.

It is also very important that the ground on which your ramp is built is completely level. If you are building a full size and costly structure it might be worth thinking about laying concrete foundations. No matter how much time you spend making a ramp level and true, on soft ground it will eventually settle and twist which you may find in time will impair your skating.

There is no need to worry about carpentry skills. A perfectly good ramp can be built using a few basic tools and the most basic skills. There are a few simple rules which should be considered when building a ramp. One is to make it *STRONG*. Reinforce every joint, where a nail will do, use a bolt or a screw. Be accurate when making measurements and particularly when cutting the transitions.

As far as tools go, you will need a claw hammer, power drill, handsaw, electric ripsaw, jigsaw, chisel, spirit level, pencil, tape measure, string and plumb line. Your materials should include ⅜" plywood for your framework and running surface and lengths of 2" × 4" timber for your crossbeams and platform construction, paint, wood glue, coach bolts, flathead nails and screws of various lengths.

So, with your materials, tools and ideas together you have the ingredients for endless hours of skating fun and creativity.

Kevin Staab,
Vancouver dawn

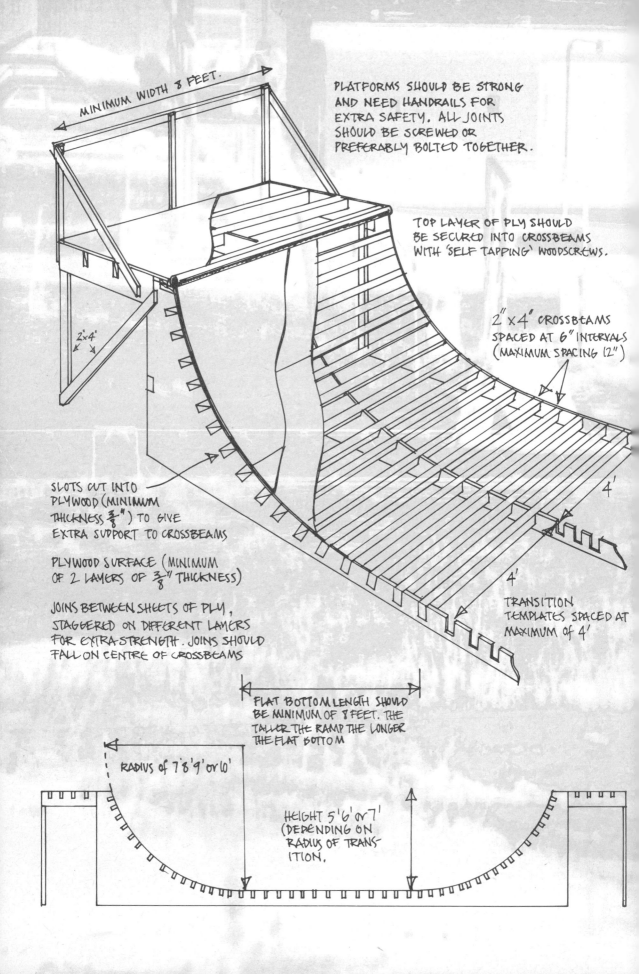

MINIMUM WIDTH 8 FEET.

PLATFORMS SHOULD BE STRONG AND NEED HANDRAILS FOR EXTRA SAFETY. ALL JOINTS SHOULD BE SCREWED OR PREFERABLY BOLTED TOGETHER.

TOP LAYER OF PLY SHOULD BE SECURED INTO CROSSBEAMS WITH 'SELF TAPPING' WOODSCREWS.

2" x 4"

2" X 4" CROSSBEAMS SPACED AT 6" INTERVALS (MAXIMUM SPACING 12")

SLOTS CUT INTO PLYWOOD (MINIMUM THICKNESS $\frac{3}{8}$") TO GIVE EXTRA SUPPORT TO CROSSBEAMS

PLYWOOD SURFACE (MINIMUM OF 2 LAYERS OF $\frac{3}{8}$" THICKNESS)

JOINS BETWEEN SHEETS OF PLY, STAGGERED ON DIFFERENT LAYERS FOR EXTRA STRENGTH. JOINS SHOULD FALL ON CENTRE OF CROSSBEAMS

4'

4'

TRANSITION TEMPLATES SPACED AT MAXIMUM OF 4'

FLAT BOTTOM LENGTH SHOULD BE MINIMUM OF 8 FEET. THE TALLER THE RAMP THE LONGER THE FLAT BOTTOM

RADIUS OF 7' 8' 9' or 10'

HEIGHT 5' 6' or 7' (DEPENDING ON RADIUS OF TRANSITION.

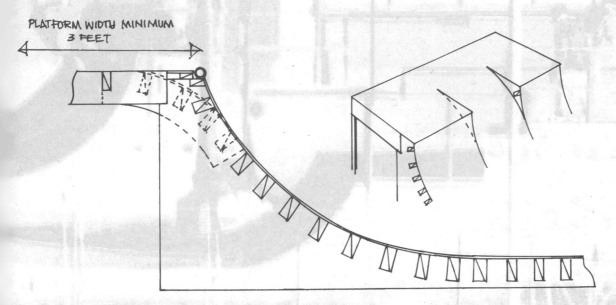

PLATFORM WIDTH MINIMUM
3 FEET

CONSTRUCTION OF ROLL IN CHANNELS AND CURVED LIPS (SIDE VIEW) △

MINIMUM $\frac{3}{8}$" PLYWOOD

LARGER HOLE DRILLED IN TOPSIDE
OF TUBING TO ALLOW SCREWS TO BE
COMPLETELY HIDDEN
SCREWS FIXED FIRMLY INTO 2"×4" CROSSBEAM

ON AN INDOOR RAMP AN EXTRA LAYER
OF HARDBOARD PROVIDES A FASTER
AND SMOOTHER SURFACE FOR YOUR
RAMP. RAMPS EXPOSED TO HARSH
WEATHER BENEFIT FROM A METAL
TOP SURFACE.

APPLICATION OF COPING (METAL OR PVC TUBING) △

ONCE THE BASIC SKILLS OF SKATEBOARD RAMP CONSTRUCTION
HAVE BEEN MASTERED A LITTLE EXTRA SPACE TIME AND
MONEY COULD LEAD TO BACK TO BACK RAMPS, CURVED
LIPS AND EVEN BOWL ENDED RAMPS. THE POSSIBILITIES
ARE ENDLESS WITH A FEW BASIC SKILLS AND SOME
IMAGINATION!

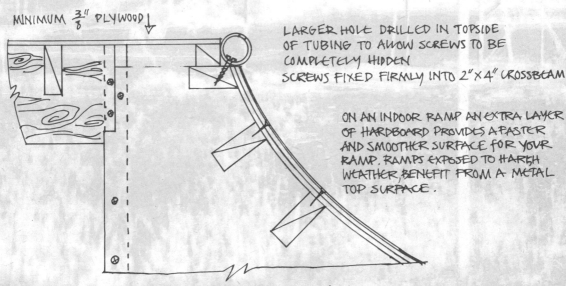

A LEVEL SURFACE IS A MUST BEFORE BUILDING
USE A SPIRIT LEVEL DURING CONSTRUCTION.

BANK	Usually short concrete or straight paved incline, often found on modern architecture. Place where rich people keep their dosh.
BAILING	A rider's deliberate loss of contact with the board, pre-empting a slam by getting off before it happens. "Knee sliding" is the definitive example of bailing. Not to be confused with the draining of pools.
BEARINGS	Small metal spheres used to prevent friction between wheels and axles. Something you lose after three McTwists.
BEANPLANT	Form of footplant, variation on a frontside boneless but grabbing the nose.
BOWL	Larger form of the cereal variety, but more fun for carving than eating your Frosties from.
CARVE	A means of travel in bowl, pool or bank with continuous foot contact on the board. Speed is sustained by constantly pushing down or up the inclines (pumping).
CHANNEL	Originally, a curved run cut into a bowl or pool but now taken to be a ramp obstacle to cross over, or not, as the case may be. Rather like the sea between England and France.
COMBI POOL	A complex of interconnecting pools. Upland was the most famous, but combi's are now a rare sight.
CONCAVE	The dip in the board when viewed from nose to tail.
CONE	Uneven wear of wheels, usually caused by slides. Thinning on the outside or inside ultimately requires said wheels to be thrown away. Not very nice.
DECK	Wooden (usually) part of skateboard (the bit you stand on) as in deck of a ship but not as in deck of cards or "I'll deck you, mate!"
DITCHES	Concrete drainage U-shaped run-offs for channelling water.
DORK	Fool or idiot. Originally derived from an abbreviation of the Surrey town of Dorking – a place of fools.
EGGPLANT	Handplant variation grabbing lip and board with opposite hands to normal invert.
ESCALATOR	Part of the lip of a ramp which usually brings two different heights together.
4 OUT BLOCK	'70s trick going up the wall, getting all four wheels out above the coping and pivoting on the tail to come back in.
FAKIE CESS SLIDE	Err . . . same as cess slide, but fakieing into it.
GRIND	On contact with a lip or kerb, trucks will usually grind, i.e. the metal axle will wear away due to friction.
HANG TEN	Boring, dated surf move, hanging ten toes over the nose of your board usually in a wheelie. Also a rather tootsey clothing company.
HIGH JUMP	As in the athletic version except that you land back on your board instead of a soft mat.
INDY	A way of grabbing the board to perform a multitude of tricks by clasping your slide rail with one hand. Brand name of hardcore trucks.
INVERT	Alternative name for a handplant.
JAPAN	Contorted frontside mute air. Originated in . . . er . . . America.
KRYPS	Abbreviation for "KRYPTONICS" skate wheel company who first produced wheels in different durometers and sizes.
LAYBACK	Leaning back so that your hand makes contact with whatever surface you're skating.
LIEN	A type of air, grabbing nose of board, often to tail. Named after creator Neil Blender (backwards).
LIP	Top of ramp/bowl/pool/bank/ditch where coping is found. Something you bite when you slam.
MADONNA	Like a lien to tail, kicking the front foot out as if to plant. Named after the horny singer. Backside version is a Sean Penn.
MINI	Smaller version of deck/ramp/car/skirt/brain . . .
MOGUL	Concrete humps like the ski equivalent. Not to be confused with press mogul Rupert Murdoch.
MUTE	A handhold on the board using the opposite hand to the one you would normally use for an indy, grabbing around the front foot.
OLLIE	The '80s street move. Invented by Alan Gelfand in a half pipe. It's a way of getting your board in the air without using your hands, just by popping the tail.
PIPES	Large concrete structures through which skaters and water move.
POWELL-PERALTA	Skate company formed by George and Stacey – well famous and not bad gear either.
RISER PADS	Plastic bits that fit between deck and truck base plates.
RUBBERS	Found in trucks, they fit on the king pin and provide suspension and turning facilities. Ask for bushings in America to avoid odd looks.
SHRED	To really rip it up.
SLALOM	Skate equivalent of ski version, i.e. a race through cones or cans set up in a course.
SLAM	An unintentional fall from your board – usually precedes pain and agony.
SMITH	Type of grind where the back truck laps over the coping and the rail of the deck touches the lip.
SNAKE RUN	First generation skate park invention. Basically a curved ditch which wriggles from side to side like a snake.
720	180 degrees more than a 540.
TOMBSTONE	Large extension from the top of a ramp to give extra vert to the adventurous or to bear an epitaph to their foolhardiness.
TRANSITION	The curve from top to bottom of any ramp or pool.
TRUCKS	Metal bits of your skateboard which enable the board to turn. Also large vehicles which make unwelcome street skating partners.
360	Early skate move in which you kick turn your board in a full circle of 360 degrees. Any turn of the board has subsequently been measured in degrees.
UZI	Small, well designed Israeli machine gun favoured by rap stars, gangsters and other unsavoury characters.
WHEELER	Travelling on one wheel.
WHEELIES	Travelling along with the front wheels in the air, not to be confused with your deckies and truckies.
W	Two "U" ramps back to back forming a "W" and enabling tricks to be attempted over the spine.
Z	Last letter of the alphabet.